wilson sat alone

wilson sat alone

by **debra hess**

illustrated by
diane greenseid

SIMON & SCHUSTER BOOKS FOR YOUNG READERS
Published by Simon & Schuster
New York   London   Toronto   Sydney   Tokyo   Singapore

SIMON & SCHUSTER BOOKS FOR YOUNG READERS

1230 Avenue of the Americas, New York, New York 10020

Text copyright © 1994 by Debra Hess. Illustrations copyright © 1994

by Diane Greenseid. All rights reserved including the right of

reproduction in whole or in part in any form.

SIMON & SCHUSTER BOOKS FOR YOUNG READERS is a trademark of

Simon & Schuster. Designed by Vicki Kalajian and Paul Zakris. The text

for this book is set in 14-point Antique Olive Nord. The illustrations

were done in Acrylic. Manufactured in the United States of America.

10 9 8 7 6 5 4 3 2 1

Library of Congress Cataloging-in-Publication Data

Hess, Debra.

Wilson sat alone / by Debra Hess ; illustrated by Diane Greenseid.

p. cm.

Summary: A little boy always does everything alone and never with

his classmates until a new girl comes to school.

[1. Bashfulness—Fiction. 2. Interpersonal relations—Fiction.

3. Schools—Fiction.] I. Greenseid, Diane, ill. II. Title.

PZ7. H4326Wi 1994 [E]—dc20   93–17616 CIP

ISBN: 0–671–87046–7

On Mondays the children in Ms. Caraway's class pushed their desks together and sat in groups of six and seven.

Wilson sat alone.

At lunchtime,
when groups of
friends ate together
in the cafeteria,

Wilson ate alone.

At recess, when everyone
gathered for a kick ball game,
or played Cowboys and Indians,
or Dinosaurs and Monsters,

Wilson played alone.

And at the end of the day, when all the children rode the bus, or climbed into cars, or wandered home in packs of three or four...   Wilson walked alone.

On reading days, while everyone clustered into groups,

Wilson read alone.

On snow days, as Ben and Sam and Lucy and Meg helped
each other into their snowsuits,

Wilson dressed alone.

When the children built snowmen, and threw snow, and
laughed and screamed, Wilson didn't laugh...

because he was alone.

One day a new girl came to school.

She said her name was Sara.

She smiled all the time.

She sat alone,
and ate alone,
and read alone,
and played alone.

But only for one day.

On her second day at school, Sara pushed
her desk into a group of other desks,

and ate with the other children,

and played Monsters in the snow,

and laughed.

And Wilson watched her from where he sat,   alone.

He watched her all that day, and all the next day, too.

And Sara saw him watching, and raced across the snow,

and roared a monster roar at Wilson,

who sat alone.

"Don't do that!" said Lucy.
"Not to Wilson," called Sam.
"Why not?" asked Sara.

"He always sits alone," said Sam.
"He always plays alone," said Meg.
"He likes to be alone," said Ben.

And then
an amazing thing happened.

Wilson roared back.

Softly at first,
and then louder,
and louder,
and louder....

It was the biggest, loudest, grandest
monster roar of all time.

And from that day on,

Wilson played with the other children,

and ate with them,

and sat with them, and read with them,

and walked with them.

And Wilson was not alone

anymore.